Princess

By Autumn Hadley Dwellings

PublishAmerica
Baltimore

© 2003 by Autumn Hadley Dwellings.

All rights reserved. No part of this book may be reproduced, stored in a retrieval system, or transmitted in any form or by any means without the prior written permission of the publishers, except by a reviewer who may quote brief passages in a review to be printed in a newspaper, magazine, or journal.

First printing

ISBN: 1-4137-0695-9
PUBLISHED BY PUBLISHAMERICA, LLLP
www.publishamerica.com
Baltimore

Printed in the United States of America

This book is dedicated to:
Arlene Ethel Davies

My Best Gifts in life
Kristie Parsons
Angela Snyder
Kelly White
Paul Nida

Jordan Taylor
Alyssa Josephine
Marana Stormee
Trinity, Sebastian, Hunter, Hailey

I Love You

Acknowledgements:
*Special thanks to
Gary Kenny
Your faith, encouragement and support became my strength as Princess Purity was given a breath of life*

*Thanks to my daughters and special friends:
Kristie Parsons and Angela Snyder: For all the hard work and long hours on this project.
Kelly White: For the time spent editing, vision and unconditional love
Robert Minke: A friend with a generous heart.
Beth Almond: For all of the advice and support.
Jim Elke: Thanks for all of your help*

Princess Purity's Journey

There was once a girl named Princess Purity, a quiet, willowy girl with creamy white porcelain skin. She wore a long, plain gown the color of ivory. She had large, dark eyes that held a deep sadness; luxurious, black, wavy hair that cascaded down her back; and a voice that carried a melody of the sweetest honey. She lived deep within the forest with her mother, Queen Kindness, and her father, King Captive.

Queen Kindness was an angelic woman with the fairest of features. She wore a sleeping gown that was soft to the touch of the skin. She had long, brown hair that draped across her shoulders; dark, deep-set eyes that danced and sparkled with life and held the sorrows of illness.

King Captive was a large man with broad shoulders, who wore clothes of only the darkest color. He had hair the color of the night sky; lines of anger embedded upon his face; eyes that penetrated the soul; a deep voice that carried for miles when he spoke; and a dark gloom that surrounded him.

The princess, Queen Kindness and King Captive lived in an ancient castle, Secret's Castle. It was worn, weathered from time and looked as if it would fall from its foundation. The windows were barred with chipped, rusted iron. Darkness hung in the air as if there was no escape.

Princess Purity was a bright girl, full of childlike innocence. She loved to daydream of dragons and princes, of winged creatures and fanciful games. She was full of life, especially in the world she created, where she could become anything her heart desired. Princess Purity watched in helplessness as her mother became very ill, disease ravaging her body, leaving her weak and frail.

"Oh, Father Captive, why must you leave in Mother's great time of need," cried Princess Purity when Father Captive disappeared to the keepers to get his own medicine.

The more he drank of this potion, the more venomous he became, spewing evil thoughts, words and deeds. She watched through child's eyes, as her world changed around her - became silent — dark.

"Father, is that you?" She sensed he was in one of his screaming rages.

"Clean this mess! Cook my meals! You're worth nothing, less than a house slave! You worthless child! Do not speak! Your words are useless. They mean nothing!"

How Princess Purity dreamed of dragons becoming bigger, princes becoming larger, winged creatures everywhere. There was limitless time in this world. Her mother's illness became more than she could bear to watch. She spent day after endless day washing, feeding, while Queen Kindness slowly withered away. Princess Purity knew deep within her heart that her mother was soon to die. As she pushed the thought away, a tear fell.

"Oh, mother, I surely shall die without you. My heart shall not bear the pain. Mother, you must get well."

She lay alone in her thoughts until she fell into a sleep. Suddenly she awoke to a loud roar. *It must be Father, home from the keepers*, she thought. As King Captive screamed louder and louder, Princess Purity sat up, frightened as he entered the room.

"Find a place to live you worthless, worthless child," said her father, "I can no longer take care of you." As he spoke, he breathed the foul stench of potion.

"But father," cried Princess Purity, "I have no one. What shall become of me?"

"I cannot be responsible for a worthless girl. Go find somewhere to stay. Get out of my sight," responded King Captive venomously.

Princess Purity ran to her room, shutting the door behind her. Her throat tightened as if someone was strangling her. Grasping for her every breath, her thoughts raced: *Where am I to go? Mother, you cannot be gone. Oh, Mother, what shall I do. Please help me.*

She longed for winged creatures to carry her off, the dragon to come with his fierce fire to fight her battles. She curled into a ball and wept, heaving in silence.

She fell into a sleep. Upon awakening, there before her stood a prince with the blondest hair and bluest eyes. Princess Purity was drawn in, as if she was looking into the ocean. He stood with an air of confidence. As she opened her eyes, she spoke, "Could I, could I be dreaming. My prince, my prince, Prince of Light; He has come. He has come to rescue me."

The Prince of Light leaned forward, touching her gently, something she had not felt before.

The princess spoke, "I am The Lowly Princess of the Forest with no place to go. I was not worthy of my father's love. I am not worthy of the prince who comes for me."

The prince gently touched her lips to silence her words of unworthiness.

"Come," said the Prince of Light.

She looked into his eyes and saw nothing but warmth - a home filled with love - magic, magic was all she could see before her. The prince picked her up in his strong arms. The princess felt the warmth of his breath as he carried her off deep into the forest.

There, before her, stood a beautiful white castle, the Castle of Dreams. She looked up captivated by the beauty that surrounded her. She was breathless. There were birds singing, flowers growing, glorious smells.

Could this be true? Is this a dream? Shall I awake to the stench of potion? she thought.

Her prince took her on journeys through the forest. Princess Purity sang and laughed, longing for this to never end. She had to touch herself to be sure this was all real. Her heart felt full and safe.

As time went on she saw the prince changing before her eyes. *Is this my gentle prince?* She could smell something on the prince when he came in from the forest and realized he was smoking the medicine plant of the forest. Hearing stories of this, she could no longer make enough food, there was laughter, laughter, laughter and then long amounts of silent slumber. She would close her eyes as if blinded by her prince.

One morning, he awoke and walked out the door. Without turning, he said, "I am taking a journey into the forest."

She waited. Days turned into nights, nights turned into weeks - then suddenly, as if out of nowhere, he appeared. Princess Purity rushed to his side.

"I thought you would never return," she said.

He turned with a cold stare and said, "My princess you must leave. We have lost everything. I have found myself a place to stay. I must leave. Farewell."

"No, No," wept Princess Purity as he turned and walked off into the distance. "My prince you cannot leave! Where shall I go? I have only you, my Prince of Light."

She ran into the castle and threw herself on the floor in complete helplessness. *I shall die without my prince.* Laying her hand on her heart she wept. The feeling of the damp, cold floor beneath her was her last thought before she slept.

Knowing she would never love again, she went out to walk among the flowers and tears fell deep from within. All of the sudden, she heard a noise that took her breath away. She looked up and there he stood - a tall, dark handsome prince with deep black eyes that hypnotized as he spoke. The deepness of his voice weakened her. The prince could sense that she was no longer sure of herself. He stepped back and spoke. "I am the Prince of Darkness. I have traveled the countryside. It has been on a long journey. I have stopped to rest. My castle, the Hidden Castle, is within two days of here."

Princess Purity wasn't sure she could speak. "May, may I offer you some food and drink?" she asked. He graciously accepted. Upon standing, the princess felt faint. She could not remember the last time she ate or slept in a warm bed. Her last memory was of a cold damp floor.

The Prince of Darkness caught her in his strong embrace and carried her into the castle. Upon entering, the coldness engulfed her. The prince laid her on the bed to build a fire. She drifted in and out of consciousness as the aroma of food circled around her.

The prince gently rested the princess's head in his arm as he slowly and lovingly fed her. After eating, she fell into a deep sleep. The prince tucked the blanket in around her. Comforted with warmth and security, Princess Purity slept a sleep as never before.

Upon awakening, she smiled. Her heart felt full. She heard the birds singing a sound that had become deaf to her ears. She lay longing to engulf the smells and sounds, asking herself, if he, the prince, had really been there, or if in her weakness, she had imagined him. Who was this stranger that disappeared as fast as he has appeared. Staring off into the distance, she dreamed of happiness. What would the future hold?

Her thoughts became only of this dark-haired, dark-eyed prince. He would appear only to tell her of her beauty and how he longed to protect her from the evils of the land. He was her knight in shining armor. When he swept her into his arms, his strength absorbed her very being. She was protected. No one could breach this barrier they created. She felt so beautiful, so alive; a glow radiated from the deepest part of her soul. *I shall be loved forever.* She was captivated in her own feeling of beauty and the warmth of her worth. Through his words she was alive. Wholeness engulfed her.

The Prince of Darkness spoke, "You must come with me to my castle, the Hidden Castle, where you shall be safe. I shall watch over you always."

He swept her into his arms as if never to let go as they rode to his castle deep in the forest. Love consumed her every breath. Nothing could touch her. They came upon an inn. The prince knew this place well. They stopped to rest and went inside. The inn was full of many people, for this was their meeting place. The princess danced, sang and laughed with the freedom of a child. Making many friends, Princess Purity longed for the night to last.

Pleasure, so much pleasure. Setting off to the side of the room, alone, her prince became restless - watching - with an intensity she had never seen before. There was darkness deep in the soul of his eyes. She trembled in silence.

"Come now," demanded the prince. "Darkness has set in. We must be on our way." The tone of his voice was urgent, edgy. She felt unsure as they rode away. The deafening silence gave her chills.

Morning set in. The excitement rose inside of her. Stretching, breathing in the fresh air, listening to the sounds of the forest, she giggled to herself.

"We shall be there soon," said the prince. She turned and kissed the prince on his cheek. No words were spoken. Sitting up straight, she saw something in the distance. Complete exhilaration overtook her. It was the castle.

Gasping, her body became rigid. She drew silent. Coldness swept over her. Drawing in a breath, she wondered what lay before her. The land was barren. Weeds and brush engulfed the castle as if suffocating its very existence. Parts of the castle were falling off the foundation. The princess choked on her tears and longed to run, run far away.

I could clear the brush, plant beautiful flowers, she thought to comfort herself. *There will be birds. It will surely be magical. I shall do this*, she told herself.

As they entered the castle, the princess looked into the

bareness; dust was everywhere; old furniture was tattered; and the smell of must overwhelmed her.

"Follow me," commanded the Prince of Darkness. They went down a long corridor until they came upon a door that was bolted from the outside. Unlocking the door, the prince spoke:

"This shall be your room." Confused, she looked around to see a single mattress on the floor.

"I, I, don't understand, my prince, there's only a place for one," she said.

"I have a room on the other side of the castle," replied the prince. "I need my privacy."

"But, but, prince," she stammered.

"Silence, silence, my princess. I shall protect you from

all." He gently caressed her face. His voice soothed her every thought. Her body felt weak. Passion filled the air. As they held each other, they drifted into a deep sleep.

When she awoke, she reached for her prince, but he was gone. There, before her, lay a tray. Leaning forward, she breathed in the aroma of freshly cooked food. What a wonderful breakfast. There before her lay a note of the finest cloth wrapped in a red lace ribbon imprinted with words of undying love:

"You take my breath away. I shall love and protect you always, my beautiful, beautiful princess.
I shall love you until death."
Forever,
Your Prince

She threw herself backward. Smiling, almost in laughter, she held herself in complete fulfillment.

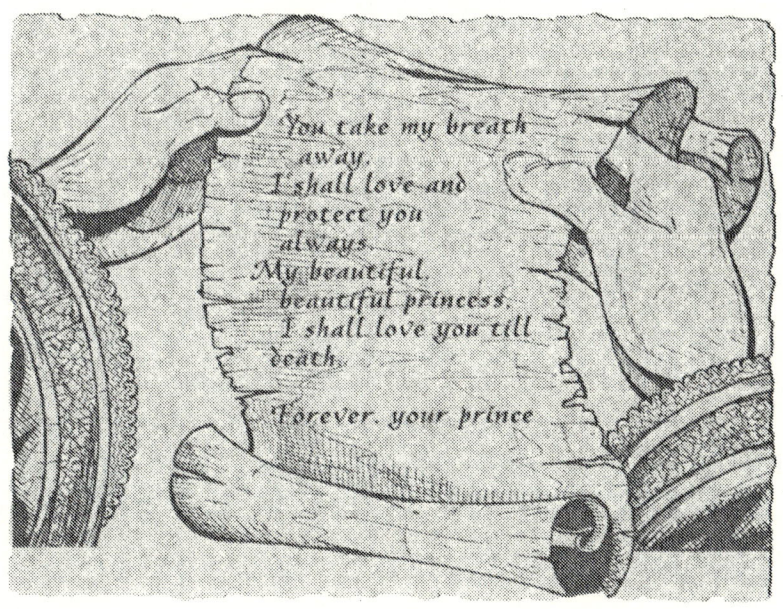

"My prince, my handsome prince," she whispered longing to shout the thought out to the world. *I must get started planting*, she thought, with a newfound exhilaration.

She began clearing the brush and thistle, anxious to plant. *Oh, how I long for the sweet smell of fresh flowers*, she thought, as dreams filled her consciousness.

As she continued planting, months passed. The princess basked in the beautiful pastel colors, sounds of birds singing filled the air; friends for the inn began to visit; and the rooms filled with laughter.

"My prince, I sense something unsettling," she said because he had become very distant - quiet.

When he spoke, his voice became very demanding, filled with coldness. "I will make you food and bring it to your room from now on," he said. "It is quiet and peaceful there."

The princess went to her room in silence, and the prince brought her food.

"You know how much I love you, my darling princess. You are all I live for," said the prince.

The princess felt a deep sadness as the prince walked away. It became hard for her to swallow her food. She felt the joy leaving her heart. *Oh, my heart hurts so*, she thought.

Day after long day the prince brought her food. As her friends from the inn came to visit her, he sent them away. "They are not worthy of you, my princess. You cannot trust them. I shall protect you. I shall never let anyone hurt you."

Twisting her arm, he threw her upon the bed. She lay stiff, unable to move — the pain unbearable. She was sure she could smell the stench of potion. The same potion her father reeked of. She lay more rigid and closed her eyes. There before her was a winged creature coming to whisk her away. There were winged creatures everywhere - dragons, wizards. *What a wonderful place*, she thought. She longed to never leave.

Then came the voice, "Tell me I am the best. I am your only prince."

Gasping for the words, she muttered, "My prince, you are the only one." Content, he passed out into a restless sleep.

Princess Purity lay silently awake, hearing every sound, every move from her prince's body. She felt cheapened, worthless — tears and more tears. Fear engulfed her soul, wrapping itself around her. Trembling, she no longer felt warmth and security. *Oh, mother, mother where are you. Hold me please*, her thoughts became loud in the silence, but were not to be answered.

The princess became lonely for her friends. She ventured out to the inn alone. She longed for laughter. Longed to feel something again, anything. She felt different as she entered the inn - lost. Her friends were overcome with joy to see her. There was hugging, kissing, laughter filled the air. She felt guilt and was uncomfortable with her own laughter.

"I must return home— my prince. I must go quickly," she said hurriedly. Everyone was saddened to see her go.

Upon arriving home, the princess dressed for sleep. As the Prince of Darkness entered, fear gripped her. She felt as if someone was suffocating her, as if she could not speak. As she turned, there he stood, grabbing her arm hard, tight.

"Where did you venture to?" asked the prince.

"I, I, the inn, my prince," replied Princess Purity. "I longed for the laughter of my friends."

The prince grabbed the princess's arm tighter, threw her across the room and shouted, "You worthless, worthless girl!" and slapped her face. "You defy me. How dare you. I warned you of these people. They are your enemies. You are never to see them again. I am the only one who truly loves you. Never, ever, defy my love for you again," warned the prince.

As he drew her into his arms and touched her, the princess grew cold, helpless.

"Forgive me, my princess," said the prince in a softer tone. "You must obey my word, and we shall be happy."

She stiffened to his touch, longing to be anywhere else. The smell of potion suffocating her. Closing her eyes the winged creatures whisked her away.

Freedom, my safe place, she thought. She felt the breeze across her face and was untouchable.

The days with the prince became unbearable as he consumed more and more potion. The princess spent many hours alone in complete silence.

The prince stood by her as she ate and berated her with repeated questions. "How is my food?" he asked over and over again.

The princess choked on every long tedious bite. She felt as if she was eating poisonous venom. She longed for him to die and thought often of committing an unspeakable act. She dreamed of burying him in the dungeon. The thoughts overwhelmed her. Days passed.

"Princess, your friends journeyed here to see you. I sent them away. I warned you. These people are your enemies. Why? Why, must you defy me? I must punish you, teach you," he said as he twisted her arm behind her back.

"I did not defy you, my prince. I haven't spoken with them. I haven't spoken with anyone. Prince, please," begged the humbled princess.

"No!" shouted the prince, "You shall stay in this room and not leave until I give you my permission."

The princess stood and raised her voice. "Prince, no! No! I will not stay in this dungeon of a room. It's dark and cold. I hate it here. Do not touch me ever again. You are an evil prince," said the princess in a moment of rallied pride.

The prince became enraged as he drew the bottle of potion to his lips and threw it across the room. He grabbed the princess and twisted her arms behind her back. "No one shall have you," he said as he threw her to the floor and spit in her face. "You shall never defy my words," he said menacingly as he slapped her face. Then, he turned, left the room and bolted the door behind him.

The princess threw herself against the door. "Let me out," she wailed, "out of this prison." The helplessness enveloped her. She lay her head in her hands, touching her face.

"Why, why is this happening?" she cried. *For I am not worthy of love. Shall I never be loved? What is wrong within me that I am not worthy? I feel as if I've been marked the lowly princess. Oh, mother, help me to understand. Help me, please. Why was father so cruel? Why could he not love me?* she thought, for in her world there was no time spent holding and rocking.

What shall I do? I have no one, she thought in a moment of panic.

Shivering from the cold breeze, the silence of the room surrounded her. She hung her head in shame. Sullen, the tears streamed down, warm to her cheeks. Her lips tasted the wetness. She was aware for a moment of complete sadness. Her heart ached with a heaviness as if it was black. In the deafening silence, she heard the sound of thumping - louder, louder - she took a breath. Would it explode? Complete aloneness introduced itself to her like a stranger in the night. She could no longer stop the tears. Her dress was soaked. The tears surrounded her feet in a puddle that raised like crystal flood water to engulf her, as her prison became an ocean. She drifted in and out of a dream state, floating on an ocean of tears. She longed to never exist in her prison.

I shall never awake, she thought as she drifted off. Exhaustion turned into a deep, deep sleep. Many hours passed as she drifted in and out.

"What? What's that sound swirling around me?" she wondered as beautiful, whimsical music moved around her as if touching her. As she listened, her soul began to dance, come alive. She heard the sound of bells off in the distance.

I see nothing, thought the princess. *Where are these bells coming from?*

Nearer and nearer, the sound of music came. She could feel the slightest little taps on her body as if some tiny little creature was walking on her.

"Where? What?" she questioned in wonderment. "Is there someone there?"

To her amazement there before her stood the tiniest little man she had ever seen. He had sea green eyes that sparkled with laughter; rosy-red chubby little cheeks so full they looked as if they would burst; the fluffiest gray hair with strands of white sprinkled throughout; and a cap and suit of gold that shimmered. He could fit in the palm of her hand.

"Who, who are you?" asked Princess Purity.

"Let me introduce myself," replied the little man. "My name is Jingles."

He was covered in all sizes of bells. He wiggled his body. The sounds of bells rung out everywhere. Out of this little man came the loudest laughter she had heard. What did it feel like to laugh, she wondered, because she could not remember the last time she had heard or felt laughter. She found herself giggling at this little man.

"My, you are the funniest little man I have ever seen," she said in a voice choked with laughter as he danced around the room.

"That's why they call me Jingles," he said as he somersaulted through mid air. Princess Purity threw her hands out to catch him as he landed.

"Jingles, where are you from? Why are you here?"

"I'm from the land of conscious. I have been with you many times. I'm here to take you on a journey."

"A journey! No! No, I cannot leave. I must not go. My prince will be angered. He shall search the land for me. I must never be out of his sight. You must go far away from here. Never come back. Please, I'm afraid for you," the princess pleaded.

"Princess Purity, don't worry over me," said Jingles disappearing as quickly as he appeared. The princess jumped to her feet.

"Where are you Jingles. Where did you go?" Bells, she heard the sounds of bells everywhere.

"Come back. Please don't leave. It's so lonely to be left alone in this cold, dark room."

Suddenly before her, there he stood. "I have gone nowhere. I have come to help you. You will be safe. I promise you this," he said as he reached out his tiny little hand.

Grasping each other they became light and music; the sound of sweet music was all she remembered. Upon waking up in a beautiful field of flowers, she heard the harmonious sounds of birds singing. Butterflies circled as she danced to a minute of joy.

"Jingles, Jingles where are you?" asked the princess.

Jingles jumped out from a patch of flowers, giggling with joy.

"Oh, Jingles, I was so afraid. Afraid you would never return."

"I shall be with you always," said Jingles . "You must take the next part of your journey alone."

"No! No!" cried the princess. "I cannot do this alone. No, Jingles, you must stay. I need you."

"Princess, you must remember, I am with you always. You must trust yourself. Follow the stream," he instructed as he disappeared.

"Jingles, Jingles," she cried as she threw herself on the ground. "I must go back to my prince. He shall protect me. I must find my home."

All of the sudden, everything around her turned to darkness. There was no color to the trees, the flowers, the grass. Frightened, she longed to scream but she had no voice. Her thoughts ran wild.

"What, what's happening? Everything looks as if it has died. There's no color left." She stood up, looking around, trembling. "Where am I?

All of the sudden, there was loud thunderous roar. Fog filled the air. There he stood, an ugly creature of a man, with his face deformed beyond recognition. He had filthy hands and claw-like discolored nails. He was dressed in black tattered rags. The princess froze as he opened his mouth as if to swallow her up and breathed out the strongest force of air she had ever felt. The breath threw her around in circles. He roared in the deepest wickedest voice, piercing her ears with its sound.

"Go back! Go back! You worthless, lowly nothing. You are useless. You ugly weak girl. You are no good to anyone. Do not fool yourself. You do not deserve to live."

The princess cringed in shame, shaking, frightened. All of the sudden, something overcame her. She thought of Jingles and of the stream. Before she knew what was happening, she started to run forward toward the stream.

Glancing back over her shoulder, she saw this creature of a man, still in the darkness screaming, "What have you ever done? You'll never make it." He screamed louder, "You worthless, worthless... ."

The princess ran faster. There, before her, lay the stream. *This must be the stream Jingles told me to follow,* thought the princess sinking on a bank to rest, gasping for breath.

She was not used to the colorless forest. It frightened her so, making her fill with sadness. She let her feet fall into the water. It was warm to the touch. She caught herself, not remembering such pleasure. Rocks and sand slid between her toes. *What a wonderful feeling*, she thought, remembering the beautiful soothing music and the bells.

She longed to hear Jingle's laughter. She missed him so. *I thought he was my friend. Oh, why did he leave me alone?* she wondered to herself.

Thoughts of his words came to her. *I am with you always. You shall be safe. You must trust yourself.* A strange peace came over her that she did not understand. She became weary as hunger set in. The princess decided to rest under a tree on the bank of the stream. She seemed to be in a dream state when he appeared - the man in black, spewing his vicious words.

"Go back, you wicked child. Rest. Who do you think you are?" He reached out to grab her with his evil claws, cutting her skin, drawing blood. "You're worthless," was all the princess could hear.

She froze, sinking down, feeling as if she had no strength to fight back. She wondered where he came from. She held herself in a fetal position, not knowing how to fight this attack on her very soul. All of the sudden, there was deafening silence.

Was he gone? Where had he gone? Would he sneak up again? She longed to no longer exist.

I hear something, she thought. The princess slowly pulled herself up. "I'm sure… ." Bells, bells. "Jingles, Jingles, is that you?" Excitement overcame her. The bells became louder and closer. She could reach out and touch the sweet sound.

It must be Jingles. She felt the little patter of feet on her body. "Jingles, Jingles, are you there?" she asked as she reached out her hand and there he appeared. He did five somersaults in mid air before he landed in the palm of her hand. "Oh, Jingles. I'm so happy to see you. My heart is full of joy. Where have you been, Jingles?"

As he wiggled his little body, the bells danced in beautiful song. "I have been on a silent journey. I have been watching over you," he said.

"Oh, Jingles. Where were you? The evil, evil man came for me. He said such terrible evil things. Jingles, I thought you were my friend. I need you," cried the princess.

Jingles leaned on his back, propping one leg over the other. "I am always here. You must remember this. When you do not see me, it does not mean I have left. Trust yourself. I am your friend. You are a worthy, beautiful princess. I believe in you."

"Jingles, I have no strength left to continue forward. I am exhausted and wary. Jingles, please stay with me while I rest."

PRINCESS PURITY'S JOURNEY

As she drifted into a deep sleep, Jingles propped himself on her shoulder. Laying his head against hers, he fell fast asleep. For such a little man, the sound of his snoring echoed deep within the forest. As the princess awoke, she saw Jingles out of the corner of her eye. She smiled in contentment.

"Jingles, I had missed you. Thanks for staying with me."

Jingles was so happy. He jumped in the air doing somersaults, singing in laughter. The sound of bells jingling consumed the air. The princess giggled. She could not stop herself. They danced, sang and laughed, overwhelmed with joy. The princess became so alive. Their hearts danced. They sat on the ground giggling.

The princess looked up at Jingles. "I feel so full of happiness when you are here. I don't feel whole without you. I am afraid to be alone."

"Princess, princess, you have many strengths. You are never alone. I am with you, within reach, just ask. If you look deep within yourself, you shall find me," said Jingles.

Jingles disappeared, but she heard the sound of bells.

Could she still be hearing bells? She followed the sound farther and farther downstream. She journeyed until, off in the distance, she heard the sound of whimsical music. The same sounds she had heard before Jingles appeared.

Could it be Jingles? Running toward the music, she cried, "Jingles, Jingles," but to her surprise, she saw a woman, stooped over tending the medicine plants of the forest.

As the princess approached with cautious and questioning steps, the woman sighted her. The woman had long, dark hair, streaked with gray; sparkling eyes that were filled with a warmth of mystery; age around her eyes and hands worn from time. She wore a radiant, flowing red cape that encircled her body. Looking at her, Princess Purity had the impression that magic would suddenly appear.

The woman looked up. "My child, calm yourself. There is no Jingles here," said the woman in the gentlest voice the princess had ever heard. "My child, you look weary and hungry as if you've been on a long journey? Come, come," said the woman. As she spoke her arms lifted into the air and a sudden gust of wind blew about. The front of her cape flew open and glorious colors filled the air. The princess began floating forward, toward the woman.

"Whoa, whoa, I'm floating," shouted the princess. "My body, it's become so light, like a feather."

As the cape covered her body, her words disappeared. Next thing she knew, there they stood in front of very small cabin. A thick smoke flowed from the chimney; birdhouses and chimes danced about, sweet aromas filled the air, there was a hand grown garden with flowers of the most glorious colors and wild animals spotted the landscape.

"Come, child," said the woman.

"I don't belong here. I live in a big castle with my prince, and he shall come for me. I'm sure of this. He promised to love me until death," said Princess Purity. As the princess talked, the woman of the forest prepared a warm bath. "I am not able to sleep here in this strange place." The princess cried for her prince as the tears streamed down her face. She dropped into the water. After the bath, the woman fixed the princess warm broth.

"Come, child, you must eat."

The princess began to eat of the broth. "What strange food this is. What is this I am eating?" asked the princess.

"It's the plants of the forest. I grow my own food, child." The princess longed to speak of the prince. The words would not come.

"This is so delicious. Thank you. What shall I call you? Do you live here alone?" asked the princess.

"My child, they call me Mystical, woman of the forest. Yes, I live here alone, but I am never alone," answered the woman.

"I, I don't understand," said Princess Purity.

"In time you will, my child. You will. Now get some rest," said Mystical as she led the princess into a room. The princess was astonished. She could not believe the sights before her. The room was magical, filled with things she dreamed of as a child: beautiful bright colors; soft, fluffy stuffed teddy bears; dolls, dolls of all sizes filled the room; big overstuffed pillows; paintings of beautiful women. She felt as if she had been there before. She slowly touched everything in sight. She stroked the dolls' hair and faces longing for something, something lost. She laid her head on her pillow and the softness of the bed engulfed her.

As she started to drift into a sleep, the princess heard a voice. "You worthless, worthless girl. You will always be the lowly princes of the forest. You are not deserving of this. You worthless girl." The tears came slowly, long, long silent tears as she fell into a sleep.

Upon awakening, she could smell the sweetest smells, hear the most soothing sounds. She dressed in the only dress the prince would allow her to wear. It was made of the darkest black, the color of coal. She buttoned up her dress looking in the mirror that lay before her. She could not believe her eyes. Touching her face, she was astonished. She no longer recognized herself. Before her was the face of a child.

"My hands, my feet, they've shrunk. They're so small," she said in amazement.

She saw the face of a child — filthy, pale, shivering, cold and alone with dark, deep set eyes and scraggly, long, black hair wearing a tattered, faded, plain, white gown.

"What's happening? I know her not," said Princess Purity. She closed her eyes refusing to see this child. She longed for her to go away. Her eyes began to blink uncontrollably. "I feel as if I'm disappearing," said the princess. "Something is happening. My hands, my feet, they're growing."

As the blinking seized, the princess felt her hands and feet. "They're normal," she said. She looked back into the mirror and touched her face. *What just happened? Who was that child?* thought the princess.

Mystical, Woman of the Forest, began to call.

"Come, my child, It is a beautiful day."

"Oh, Mystical, my prince shall come to save me. He has promised to let no harm come to me. He shall be very angry. You must fear him," warned the princess, trembling as she spoke.

"My child, you are safe. Calm yourself. What do they call you?"

"I am Princess Purity, the Lowly Princess of the Forest. I am not worthy of love. I was not worthy of my father's love," replied the princess.

"Princess Purity is a lovely name. You are a beautiful princess worthy of so much love. You will come to believe this in time. Come, I have a wonderful meal prepared," said the older woman. As the princess ate she remembered the prince standing over her, berating her while she ate, the food becoming harder and harder to swallow with every bite.

"I must leave now - my prince," said the princess nervously.

"Come, my child," soothed Mystical. She led Princess Purity into a room filled with crystals that sparkled about; flickering candles dancing around; and whimsical music in the air. The sweet aroma of burning plants of the forest calmed her senses. Mystical had the princess lay on a bed of feathers covered in the finest cloth. She sank. Unsure, as she lay waiting, she heard Mystical's voice. She was whispering, "Gently, breathe deep within yourself, hold, then release." The princess followed the instructions. She sank deeper and deeper into sleep. The sweet sound of music soothed her. She drifted to a wonderful place.

It was as if she drifted into a trance-like sleep. She longed to stay forever. Mystical gently guided her back. The princess rubbed her eyes as if awakening from a long sleep.

"Oh, Mystical I long to go back to this place," said the princess in a sleepy voice.

"Princess, we have plenty of time," said Mystical. She pulled out a beautiful, wooden, hand-painted box. The princess looked up in surprise, disbelief.

"Is this for me?" she asked. She began to cry. Inside were five stones of different colors. "Oh, Mystical, thank you. They're so beautiful."

"Princess Purity, carry these close to your heart. You shall use them on your journey," said Mystical.

The older woman taught her of the healing plants of the forest and told stories into the dark of the night. The princess sang, danced, and forgot herself in the moment. As the night ended, she dresses for bed. Filled with warmth and contentment, she clutched the stones close to her heart.

"Could this be real? It frightens me so."

Confused, she drifted into a peaceful sleep. She awoke, startled by her own screams. It was the prince. He's come to capture me. Her body trembled in fear as if he was in the room breathing onto her. *I must be dreaming*, she thought as she jumped to her feet, her body rigid, shaking as she wept. "I am shaking, so what's happening to me? I feel so alone. Take away my suffering. Help me, please," she cried as she threw herself across the bed.

I shall always be nothing more than The Lowly Princess of the Forest, not worthy of happiness. I shall die as a lowly wretch. Shall I be saved? Surely, there is a prince on his way to rescue me, whisk me off into his strong arms to a beautiful place where I will be loved and cherished forever. She was sure of this as she drifted off into a fitful sleep. She awoke feeling dread upon her.

Mystical sensed that something was bothering the princess. "You don't look well this morning," said the Mystical. "Drink this, my princess." Tears started to fall from the princess's eyes, big tears. The more she wept the larger the tears.

"My child, my child, what is your ailment?" said Mystical.

"I know not what ails me," was all Princess Purity could

say. She threw herself into Mystical's arms, "Oh, Mystical," she said sobbing so hard that her whole body heaved. "It's the prince. I dreamed he came for me. His evil presence was upon my body, stealing my soul. If he can not have me he shall take my heart. I fear him so. He terrifies me. I was forbidden to laugh in his kingdom. I was terrified to speak. He berated me, only allowed me to eat alone or in his presence. He let me know no one shall ever, ever desire me, that I am the lowly princess that I am, truly marked. I must look upon him as the King of his castle, never defy his words," blurted the princess choking on her tears, her voice trembling. "I am so afraid."

"My princess, my sweet princess, you are safe here," said Mystical as she stroked her hair. Mystical's voice was soothing to the princess. "I must walk to the stream," said the princess as she lifted herself to go.

"My child," said Mystical, "I shall be here upon your return."

While walking to the stream, the princess was in deep thought. *I should have never spoken of my prince to Mystical. I have deceived him. He shall never trust me. He shall punish me terribly. I must leave. He shall surely find me here. I am afraid for Mystical's life.* As Princess Purity sat by the river she felt so alone within herself.

A prince, any prince, shall surely save me from this fate worse than death, she thought. The princess sat in complete silence. "I shall walk to the stone bridge ahead. Oh, Mystical, I shall miss you so," she said as she started down stream. "What, what's happening?"

Suddenly, the water started stirring around her feet, faster, faster, "Whoaaaaaa, whoaaaaa, what's happening?" Her body swayed back and forth. The water stirred up faster and faster, pulling her under. It sucked her through a small hole to the other side of the bridge. Her head surfaced above water. She gasped. As she opened her mouth, water flew everywhere. When she opened her eyes, she could not believe what a beautiful, wondrous sight lay before her. It was the land of serenity, glorious, glorious colors.

Is this really happening? she thought as she opened and closed her eyes again.

She swam to the shore. She took a deep breath. She could not believe the aromas in the air. Birds singing, animals everywhere. She ran all around, swam, lay under the warmth of the sun. All of the sudden, the deepest dread filled her being.

The voice came, "You're worthless without a prince. You do not deserve such glory. Leave now."

She looked around in wonderment. *Surely, someday I shall be worthy of such beauty, a prince that shall love and cherish me*, she thought. She leaned forward breathing in all the freshness, touching everything because she knew she had to leave.

As she turned, there he stood, The Prince of Darkness. Drawing in a deep breath, she froze in silence, strangling on her own voice. The Prince of Darkness grabbed her arm and screamed, "You worthless, useless wretch of a girl." The princess tried desperately to pull her arm away. He grabbed her up, screaming, "You defied me! You shall never leave my sight and shall be punished harshly for this. You are nothing but the Lowly Princess of the Forest. No one shall have you. It is only I who shall have you, until death!" He grabbed her face. "Look at me while I speak," he demanded.

The princess cast her eyes to the ground in shame. She trembled uncontrollably. Tears of shame slowly caressed her cheeks. "My prince, oh please, forgive me, I shall obey your every word. Without you surely I shall cease to exist. I shall never be worthy of your love, my prince," said the princess

"Do not speak!" shouted the Prince of Darkness. "We must leave now," he commanded as he threw her upon his horse.

The princess could no longer speak. Her thoughts consumed her. *My heart is pounding, beating so fiercely*, she thought. Beads of sweat poured down her body. *What shall I do?* she thought as her eyes longingly roamed every beautiful sight as they rode off into the darkness. For the princess there was no time. Hours turned into days, days turned into night. The rain did not cease. A cold chill filled the air. The princess became so cold her body shook. Surely, the wetness had pierced her skin and gone deep within her lungs. Aching and trying desperately not to breathe in the cold air, her jaws aching from clenching them so tightly.

Surely I shall die alone in this dark forest with this beast of a prince, she thought. *It is so cold and dark. Where shall I go? How shall I leave? I must find a way. Someone, please, help me.*

All of the sudden, there was a roaring sound like nothing ever heard before. The trees shook; lightning cracked. The wind roared, throwing the prince far, far off into the distance. Another gust picked up the princess. She went tumbling through the air, limbs, leaves and sticks circling about her.

"What, what's happening," she said out loud. "Whoaaaaaa, whoaaaaa," then there was complete darkness. Something set her down.

"It's, it's so dark. Where am I? What's happening? Who's there?" she said.

Upon standing, she became lightheaded and dazed. "My hands, my feet, my body, they're so small, my voice barely recognizable," she said. Her voice was the voice of a child. "Go away. Leave me alone," cried the princess.

"I long to go home," she cried. She realized she had no home. Not knowing what home felt like her eyes began to blink, faster and faster. Her thoughts spun. She shrieked, "I'm disappearing. My hands, my feet, they're normal again," she said. She suddenly realized that the strange filthy child was back. "I'm so confused. What does she want? My prince," she cried, falling to her knees in despair.

All she could do was weep with such intensity that her body shook and heaved uncontrollably. It seemed as if hours had passed. Her body was so tired she could hardly move. As she drew herself to a kneeling position, she looked into the darkness. She no longer recognized who was there — if anyone was there. She saw light twinkling in the sky.

"Oh, my heart hurts so. Please hear my cry. I know not love. Please send arms to comfort me in my despair, and aloneness. My heart is burdened so. Do you hear my cries?"

The princess knelt in silence. The twinkling faded. The darkness coveted her soul. Weary from exhaustion, she slept. She was awakened by a rustling sound in the distance. Fear crept over her.

"Who's there. Who's there? Please answer," she asked in the darkness. Silence was the only answer. "Is someone there," she questioned again.

There, before her, stood a faceless man emanating a white glow from underneath a black hooded cape.

"Who are you?" asked the princess longing to run. Her feet would not move. "Why are you here? Please don't hurt me. I'm waiting for a prince who I know not to rescue me form this darkness," she said.

The faceless man just stood, waiting. "Why don't you speak?" asked the princess. "I am lost in this dark forest. Which way shall I go?"

Eerie silence was all she could hear. "I know a prince, any prince shall rescue me," said Princess Purity to the man standing statue-like before her. "I must wait. Who are you? You're scaring me. Please, speak to me."

"I am Shadow, Father of Enlightenment," said the man roaring with wicked laughter as his breath hissed threw the air.

"Follow me," he said through more dark laughter. "Do not fear me. Trust me," he said. The sound of his breath filled the air. As he reached for her hand, the princess felt a strange energy force pulling her toward this dark presence.

"I mustn't go," she meekly whispered, as her hand fell into his, and she became disoriented.

"Where are you taking me?" she asked.

Shadow answered her with a silent pause. "Follow," was all he finally said.

As she followed Shadow, she could only see glimpses ahead. It seemed as if they trudged through the woods for hours, following some sort of path. With a sudden jolt, Shadow turned to face the princess. There was a light so bright emanating from him she had to step back as not to be blinded. Before her lay a vast open field covered with the magical mushrooms of the forest. Stories told they were to be found only after a rain.

"Ahahaahahahahahahahah," roared Shadow. "Welcome to the Land of Illusion. Go, now, my princess. Take of these mushrooms, ahahahahahahahah. They shall take away your suffering. Trust me, ahahahahahaha."

A strangeness engulfed her as the force led her into the field.

"There are, there are, so many. Which one shall I try?" she asked. Before she realized it, she had eaten three.

"Oh, my, I'm dizzy. I feel as if I shall faint," she said in a shaky voice. Shadow's laughter surrounded her. Fear engulfed her as she drifted in and out of consciousness. "Shadow, where are you?" she asked.

"Ahahahahahahaha," was all she heard.

Her body began to spin uncontrollably. She could not stop as brilliant colors encircled her. Reaching through their transparency, she heard beautiful sounds, the animals of the forest singing. All of the sudden, as if from no where, the spinning ceased. The princess tried desperately to catch her balance, falling backwards before catching herself on her hands. She felt something awful.

"My stomach, it aches so," she said. There were snakes, snakes, hundreds of snakes surrounding her. Fright stole her voice. She was afraid to breathe for they might strike with poisonous venom. She was unable to control the trembling.

Before she could take a breath, there he was, Cobra, the king of all snakes, ready to strike his victim. The princess was paralyzed with fear. Cobra struck her throat with such powerful force it threw her backwards. No longer able to speak or swallow. She slowly rolled on her stomach. Her skin began to change as if it were melting away from her body.

Death was surely upon her. She must get away from here. She was no longer able to stand. Leaving her skin behind, she slithered away deeper into the forest. Becoming weaker and weaker, she sat under a big tree so full it shadowed her from the sun. Her body began to shake uncontrollably. She began to vomit. Unable to move, the pain coursed through her raw body. Her vision began to blur. As darkness took over, days passed.

"I must make it to the stream," said the princess who was barely able to move as she slowly crawled through the dirt and brush tearing at her body.

"I must not stop. I must make it to the stream," she

sputtered as she collapsed upon the bank, she heard a sweet gentle voice.

"Oh, Mystical, Mystical, is that you?" she asked as she wept.

"Yes, my sweet princess," said Mystical as she drew her up into her arms.

"I feel as if I am dying," said the princess. "I am so weak. I can no longer go on. Oh, Mystical, I have no strength left to continue on this journey. Please help me to suffer no longer, Mystical, please."

"My beautiful princess," soothed Mystical as she gently stroked the princess's hair. "Drink of this tonic. You must rest."

"Stay with me Mystical, please, you must not go. I need you. I cannot be here alone," said Princess Purity.

"I shall stay with you as you regain your strength," said the older woman.

"Thank you, Mystical," whispered the princess as she slowly closed her eyes.

Mystical washed the princess's body with the medicine plants of the forest. As the princess continued to drink of the tonic, new skin began to form. Mystical reached into the princess's gown to retrieve the five stones she had given her for they now carried a special healing energy. She soaked them in a water mixture from the forest. She encircled their bodies with the stones as she chanted songs of healing. The princess began to regain her strength.

"I must continue on my journey," said Mystical.

"I wish you not to leave," said Princess Purity as the tears began to fall. "My heart hurts so. I am so weak within. I shall not survive."

"My princess, my princess, you shall live. You have many strengths. You must look upon these," said Mystical as she handed the princess a necklace made of the finest crystal.

"Wear this close to your heart," instructed the older woman, filling it with warmth.

"Oh, Mystical, I shall cherish this forever. Thank you, thank you."

"I must go," said Mystical. As she walked off into the distance, the princess sat in silence embracing the necklace to her heart.

"I shall never release you," she said as she pulled herself up to continue on her journey. She gained strength from Mystical's teachings. She made her own salves and tonics, chanting as she continued on her way. Suddenly, she came to so many paths in the forest that she became overwhelmed.

"Which way shall I choose?" she wondered frantically. She became lightheaded. Colors flashed before her. "Oh, no!" The spinning - the aftertaste of mushrooms filled her mouth. With great effort the princess steadied herself. There was a deafening silence.

"Where am I," said the princess, her eyes widening. There, before her, stood the Soul Stealers, the tiniest little men with the sharpest teeth she had ever seen. Surely they were friendly, she thought, longing to talk to anyone. She walked forward and leaned over to speak to them.

"Why, hello," she said. "I am the Lowly Princess of the Forest. I have lost my way in search of my prince. I'm not sure he shall find me. I have journeyed a long way. Would you please help me find my way out of the dark forest?"

"Princesses, princesses, princesses," squeaked the tiny little men in their wicked little voices. "We hate princesses. We eat them," they screeched as they started piercing her skin with their razor sharp teeth.

I must run as fast as I can, thought the princess. She ran through brush, thistle, sticks and thorns, tearing at her flesh, drawing blood. She ran faster and faster, not stopping until total exhaustion took over.

Princess Purity fell upon a clearing, a beautiful green river bank adorned with flowers of every color and smells that touched every sense in her body. "How long had it been since she really breathed?" she wondered. The sounds of music filled her ears as the tears slowly started to fall. She looked down at the black, tattered gown the prince had chosen. It was her only gown. As she touched the bleeding cuts, a sadness filled her heart.

"Who is this person?" she wondered. "Why must you hurt so? I am so sorry for you. I would like to help you."

The tears began to fall harder as she tore part of her dress. She longed for the water against her body. As she dipped the cloth into the water, suddenly the princess recognized the reflection of a child, the same child she had seen in the mirror at Mystical's house.

"You are so weak and filthy," she whispered, ignoring the child. She gently wiped the blood from the open wounds. "Why is this happening," she said as her eyes searched the sky. "Why must I suffer so? Shall I ever trust again, ever be truly loved? I only ask to be held close, feel warmth. I long to be safe. Shall any one ever love me like this? My heart hurts so. I must sleep."

The princess lay her head upon the grass to sleep. Tears falling as she whispered ,"Oh, the star that glows so very bright, I wish to be loved," as she drifted into a sleep.

Upon awakening, the princess was afraid to open her eyes for surely this was only a dream. She sat up with a start as if forgetting something. Was she hearing bells? No, it could not be. She drew in a breath, suddenly filling with excitement.

"Jingles, Jingles, is that you? It cannot be Jingles. He disappeared. He's forgotten me." Loud bells began to jingle everywhere.

"Ha, what, forgotten you?" he said as he somersaulted through the air. "Forgotten you? Never."

"Well, where have you been? Jingles, you promised you would always be there. I, I, I, was almost killed - snakes, snakes, evil little men," she tried to explain, stumbling over her words, "and, and, magical mushrooms."

"Whoaaa," said Jingles, "slow down."

"I am exhausted," said the princess. "Jingles, I missed you, so. It saddens my heart when you disappear. You promised you would be with me always."

"You must call upon me," said the little man.

"Oh, Jingles, I am so confused. Shall my heart ever stop hurting? I love all the evil princes. I feel as if I am blind. Shall I ever find the right prince, ever find a warm, safe, home or ever be worthy?"

"You are a beautiful princess. Look deep within. Trust yourself. You have always been worthy," said Jingles.

"Oh, Jingles, my heart is so full. You bring me so much laughter and happiness," said the princess.

Jingles jumped up and down, his bells jingling with such sound. It sounded as if a symphony surrounded them. He giggled, doing somersaults as the princess sang, her voice carrying the sound of the sweetest honey. She could not believe her own ears.

Weeks passed.

"Oh, Jingles, stay with me. I am so happy. I never know how to laugh with anyone else," she said.

"I must go now. I shall be watching over you. I am within. Trust yourself," he said.

"Jing------gles," before she could finish, he was gone. She searched all around.

"Jingles, Jingles, don't go. I cannot do this alone." The princess began to sing to comfort her broken heart. Her voice echoed deep into the woods to the cabin of the prince known throughout the land as The Wood Prince. He could smell her tears. "I must find the princess with the voice of honey," he said as he journeyed into the forest.

The princess sang herself into a deep sleep. Upon awakening, there he stood, The Wood Prince. He had a strong build. He was stocky in appearance with sandy, curly hair, soft to the touch. She felt the warmth of a touch so gentle she was sure it came from a small child. He had a voice so reassuring it cradled her heart with comfort; eyes that melted her soul with desire, a desire she had never known. He lifted her gently in his arms, carrying her into his cabin, into the dark of a flickering light. He tucked her in. He caressed her cheeks with the warmth of his touch and ran her hair through his fingertips ever so slightly. Her heart was filled with the innocence of a child as she drifted into a deep sleep.

Upon awakening, she knew their souls had met. This was her prince. She would be with him always, until death. They talked of sharing lifetimes together. He was different from the other princes. He crafted birdhouses from wood and hung chimes and crystal glass throughout that sang whimsical music to the soul. The sun would shine through the crystal with such brilliance the colors danced upon your skin. He was music to her soul.

He never forced himself upon the princess.

She whispered words of praise as she silenced him. The prince reached for Princess Purity, pulling her close until their bodies were wrapped within each other and whispered words of her beauty. With only the flickering light and sweet music in the air surrounding them, the prince drifted into a sleep. The princess could not believe the magic. The child within herself, protected from all evil. She could giggle and share her most secret desires. She had never before felt such deep emotion. Every day brought a new warmth, security. Nothing else existed outside their world. The prince brought her many magical gifts. Her heart was filled with the warmth of a child. The prince would play his musical instruments. They would sing - laugh. She would fall into his arms as they danced to the music that surrounded them.

Upon awakening, she felt the prince's lips brush across her cheeks. The warmth of his breath cradling his desires.

"I must go into the forest for 14 days," he whispered as his fingers gently touched her lips. "I have business to tend to. I shall return. You shall be safe," he said as he laid his hand on her heart. She could feel the strength from his words of love.

Searching for her hand, he pressed it against his heart. "I shall carry you here, always," he said as he pulled her into his chest. Their mouths met with such passion that there was no time. While the prince was away, the princess journaled thoughts and dreams; hopes and desires. Dancing under the moonlight, her heart filled with desire, and she thought of painting beautiful pictures. Laying still in her thoughts by the flicker of candlelight, laughter filled her with the voice of a child.

"Oh, my prince. I love him so. I feel as if I'm the most beautiful princess in the forest," she sang.

She heard a knock. *Who could this be*, she thought as she opened the door. It was the messenger, a tall, sturdy man with a deep, steady voice; a reassuring smile; and large hands covered with gloves, wearing a neatly defined uniform of the finest material and a cap tilted slightly forward, carrying himself in the most professional manner.

"Please, come in, sit," said the princess as he entered.

"I have been on a long journey. Do you mind if I drink of the potion I bring with me?" asked the messenger

"You must respect the prince, does he let you drink of this potion?" queried the princess.

"Why, yes, the prince has consumed with me - many times," said the messenger.

"I, I, don't believe this. It mustn't be true. You must leave. You must be mistaken," said the princess.

"I am sorry princess. I speak the truth. I shall be on my way." As he shut the door behind him, the princess slid to the floor.

"No!" she wailed. "No, this is not true. This is not happening, not my prince. I shall ask him upon his return."

The days and nights became long and dark. She was consumed with the worry of how she would approach him. She spent restless nights of wondering, longing for it to be untrue. The princess readied herself on the day of his return and longed to be in his arms again. She could sense him approaching. As he entered, excitement enveloped her. The sight of him took her breath away. She threw herself in his arms, all thoughts eluding her, as the prince carried her off passionately. Days passed as they lay in each other's arms, enraptured by the moment.

"I must speak to you my prince," said Princess Purity. "The messenger came while you were away. I believe he spoke an untruth. I must know my prince. Do you consume of the potion?" His body stiffened as he drew himself up.

"Yes, my princess. I do consume of potion."

Her heart sank in deep despair. She gently touched his face. "I shall love you always, my prince," she said as she comforted him.

Days passed, and the prince began to consume more and more of the potion. The princess smelled an aroma she thought was familiar.

"My prince, what is the aroma I am smelling?" she asked.

"It is the medicine plant of the forest," he answered. A sadness engulfed her. Her heart sank as she watched her prince. Fear consumed her. What was happening?

As she drifted in her thoughts, there was a knock at the door. It was the messenger returning. "I have brought you a message from the Land of Memory. Your previous princess, Princess Turmoil, sends you an urgent message: *Your son Bewildered shall be arriving soon. Princess Turmoil can no longer tend to him. If you do not receive him, he shall be thrown into a dungeon. He is in much trouble. He consumes of potion, and the medicine plants of the forest.*" The prince paid the messenger and sent him on his way.

The princess, longing for a family, thought, *I shall love him for he is part of my prince.*

When he arrived, The Wood Prince's son was extremely thin and would not eat. He was frail in appearance and looked as if he'd disappeared upon a glare. His blue eyes held an uncertainty as if he was lost within himself.

The prince became consumed with guilt, frustration and anger. The princess became quiet, her heart aching, longing for her prince to return again - the prince that sang and dance and played music - for he was slowly disappearing. The prince's son became like an infant, sleeping days away. The prince became angrier and angrier, yelling, "I cannot get Bewildered to work. He does nothing with his time."

The princess tried to comfort the prince to no avail. As the days went on, the prince became distant, shutting everyone out, only wanting to spend time with Bewildered. The princess went off alone - walking, afraid to stop - afraid that the pain would consume her, and she would lay down and die.

Morning came upon them as the prince said, "I need to talk to you. I must spend my time with Bewildered. You must go away. I shall see you only once a month."

The princess gasped for air as she ran into the forest. She ran faster, faster, her chest hurting with every breath she took until she came upon Kingdom Castle. A great towering castle, majestic in appearance, that looked deserted but well kept. There were windows of glass filled with colors that radiated a beautiful hue.

As she entered, she was taken aback. The beauty captivated her. The castle was filled with pictures of transparent women adorned with majestic wings - women in beautiful silk robes, a picture of a male with a halo of thorns wracked in pain as if he had suffered greatly. She had heard stories of this great man. He carried love and forgiveness for all that seek him. The women were angelic in stature. The princess fell to her knees and wept.

Looking up in awe, she begged, "Please, please do not take away my prince for he is the only one I have truly loved.

My heart hurts so. Please do not take away what you have given me. Why, why would you torture me so? I have already suffered so. My prince is a great gift. Please you mustn't take this away."

As she wept, before her lay many candles. *I shall light one for the prince and his son and others who suffer so.* She left the place, longing to stay. The princess journeyed into the forest not far form The Wood Prince's castle. She lay on the hard ground to sleep

I feel so alone, she thought. *This ground is hard and cold. Oh, my prince, how I long for you.* She stayed months in the forest and tried desperately to talk with her prince. He grew warm and cold.

"I shall surely die from the pain that racks my body," cried the princess. The only thing that kept her alive was the faith she drew from Kingdom Castle, the castle of her retreat. She would fall to her knees before this great man and angelic woman, her heart aching for her prince.

"I come to you unworthy. I am nothing. I know not love. How could you, this great man of love and forgiveness, love me, the lowly, wretched princess of the forest? I am nothing."

As she threw herself down, weeping, a voice of rage came out of her that she did not recognize.

"I despise my father so. He has stolen my soul and broken my heart. I long for my mother. Oh, please forgive me. Comfort my heart."

As she turned she saw a giant of a man in a flowing white robe with strong features; a voice that transpired the deepest of knowledge; and a warmth surrounding him sharing visions of truth.

"Who are you?" Princess Purity asked startled.

"Come, my child, sit, my name is Spirituality. I have been told that you have come in search of me, that your journey has been filled with pain and suffering."

Something came over the princess, and she poured her soul to this man for he did not judge her. He spoke of great miracles of the heart and of forgiveness. The princess continued to sleep on the hard cold ground of the forest. Her prince became very cold and angry. She felt as if death was upon her. Sleep eluded her as she tried desperately to hold on to her prince.

The prince sent a messenger into the forest to retrieve her. When she heard the prince would soon leave the land, her heart filled with dread. As she entered the Wood Prince's castle, he spoke, "My heart lay heavy with despair. I must leave this land to start a new life."

The princess felt betrayed. All of his words of love filled her thoughts. *He told me I would be with him always*, she thought. "Please, my prince," she cried. "I shall never exist without you. I was so safe and protected. My heart shall never bear this loss."

He took her in his arms and held her and comforted her heart with promises of messages and journeys to be with him. "You shall always be part of my life," he said as he took her in his arms. "I desire you." The princess could not bear to loose him to a strange land. The pain of the loss was so great, she left part of herself closed off in the distance, not to be touched.

As the months passed her heart saddened while she waited for a message from the prince.

"What had happened?" she wondered. She found herself in Kingdom Castle more and more, lighting candles. She knelt before the angelic women.

"Oh, teach me to be loved. If you hear my words, teach me how to forgive and be forgiven, so I may love and forgive others. Teach me to comfort where there is no comfort. I come to you with nothing before me. Guide me please. Maybe my prince is not what you desire for me. Please show me the way. I am lost," she prayed.

Time passed before the princess had finally sent word to her prince. She wept and was filled with angry words of his broken promises. They sent messages back and forth. Messages of her longing and no longer wanting to be without him. Then nothing from the prince. He denied her very existence. Anger filled the princess as the tears fell. She thought she would drown in her own sorrow for she knew she must send the prince a final message.

"My prince this shall be my last message." She knew she must keep this promise to herself, and she no longer sent messages to the prince.

The princess journeyed to Kingdom Castle to find Spirituality. As she entered, there he knelt.

"I was expecting you," he said as she knelt beside him. "I have brought you a gift of great perfection," he said as he opened his hand. She sat in silence.

There, before her, lay a wafer white as snow, sparkling as if it was made of the finest gold. The princess knew of no other gift that could be so sacred. She must eat of this wafer. As she lifted her head slightly, she opened her lips as he lay the wafer upon her tongue. She felt a warmth within her soul, embracing her heart. She knelt before the great man of thorns and wept as never before.

Upon leaving, she lit candles for everyone that had ever journeyed in her path. The princess journeyed back into the forest before night fell. She knew the day that lay before her was full. She must find work.

As the weeks passed, she was pleased to find work reading many wondrous stories to the ill and injured of the forest.

She received many gifts of wisdom in return. She found herself thinking of the prince less, for she knew he no longer belonged to her. She must journey forward.

As she ventured deeper into forest, she stopped dead in her tracks. The ground shook. There was a loud deafening thunderous roar. Fog encircled her. There he stood, the ugly creature of a man dressed in black with filthy, claw-like hands and foul smelling breath.

"So, you thought you'd get away from me, you weak, ugly, worthless girl," he said. His breath knocked her to the ground. "You won't get away this time."

Strength overcame the princess as she drew herself up. "I know who you are. I am worth something," she said as he roared louder and louder.

"You shall never do this alone. Without a prince you are a weak failure," he spewed.

The princess stood firm as his breath grew fouler and fouler.

"I am never alone," she shouted.

Suddenly, something strange started happening. The creature started shaking uncontrollably, spewing out vicious words everywhere until he became speechless, and slumped to the ground.

"Oh, my," said the princess as his claws began to shrink, the filth on his hands began to disappear. His clothes were no longer black and tattered. His face began to take on human features resembling the princess's father, King Captive, only kinder and gentler. His voice began to soften.

"I would like to be your friend," said the princess as she reached out her hand. "Please join me," she said as they embraced.

The princess continued on her journey, stopping to bath in the river along the way. She lay under the stars from the night sky. The princess heard a rustling sound.

"Who's there?" she asked. But, she received no answer. "Who's there?" she asked again.

Then came the sound of wicked laughter: "Ahaahahahahahahaahah." It was Shadow, Father of Enlightenment. She could see the light illuminating from under his hood. "Hahhahahahahahahahaha you thought you could hide from me," taunted Shadow. "Trying to pretend I did not exist, you foolish girl."

"I am not foolish. I am not hiding from you," said the princess. She could hear his eerie breathing as he reached out his open hand.

"I have brought something for you, my princess," he said, "to help you forget your suffering."

There, in his hand, lay the biggest magical mushroom the princess had ever seen. The size surprised her so. It threw her off balance, and she started to sway back and forth. She heard Shadow's wicked laughter.

"My princess have some. Try a little taste," said Shadow.

"No," shrieked this little voice. "No, no, no, no!" she continued, her voice becoming louder and louder. The louder her voice, the steadier her body became, until she was standing firm.

"No," she roared so loud that Shadow began to tremble. He shook so fiercely that he fell to the ground. His mouth opened and suddenly the fog that surrounded him began to disappear. With every breath he inhaled, he sucked in more fog until it completely filled his being. His light became brighter and the princess realized the light no longer blinded her. She could look right into Shadow. He looked as if he would explode as the princess spoke. "I would like to be your friend," she said.

Suddenly, something began to happen. As Shadow, opened his mouth, his body took on different shapes. Then a sudden gust of air shot out of his body in a magical dance that surrounded the princess's body, reaching, touching. The beautiful light that emanated from his breath suddenly turning into a great ball of light that danced on the princess's fingertips.

Her voice filled with the softness of a feather floating in time. "I accept you. Please, join me," she said. As she spoke these words, the light swooped up and entered her body filling her entire soul. She felt a peace within that she had never experienced before. She fell into a silent sleep for what seemed like days.

Upon awakening, she spoke, "My heart, my heart feels so much lighter as if it shall float away. I, I can smile," she said as she touched her lips to be sure she was not deceiving herself. *I feel stronger*, she thought in wonder.

As she stood up to continue on with her journey, not knowing what lay ahead, she skipped and sang and danced to memories of such sweet music. As her heart fluttered to the sounds, she no longer recognized her surroundings. A familiar feeling came over her.

"Where am I. I am lost," she said. Rustling sounds filled the air. The patter of little feet surrounded her with a fury. "I recognize you! Why, you're the little men of the forest, The Soul Stealers."

They became furious hearing this. They began squeeking, "Princesses, princesses, we hate princesses." They opened their mouths wide, bearing their razor sharp teeth.

"You shall never get away with this. We shall devour you," they threatened.

The princess shouted, "I know who you are. You are the Stealers of Souls. You have come to steal my soul, you tiny, evil, little men."

Hearing this made them more enraged than ever. Their breath became hot as fire. As they shrieked louder and louder, they began to grow larger and larger. The princess suddenly remembered the special vial of oil Spirituality had given her to protect her from The Soul Stealers. She grabbed for the vial, breaking the seal quickly.

I must remember the words he taught me, she thought. As she spoke the words, she threw the special oil all over the vicious little men.

Something strange began to happen, the little men began to scream. Their bodies began to shudder and shriek. Their breath became cold. Their razor-sharp teeth shrinking smaller and smaller, until they lay in a heap of dust on the ground before her.

"You shall never steal my soul," she said, looking down at the dust at her feet.

In one swoop, the dust circled round forming the figure of an ancient man named Clarity. He had a long white beard and hair that drug the ground and he grasped a walking stick made of the old wood of the forest. He had strong firm hands, wrinkled from time, eyes that were worn and yet sparkled with the knowledge of life.

The princess drew nearer and reached out her hand. "Welcome, please join me on my journey," she said. He lay his hand upon hers. Suddenly she felt a great warmth within, her thoughts become alive, filled with a knowledge she had never known.

"My eyes, my eyes, they feel so different. Everything

seems brighter, more colorful, alive. I can see so clearly," she said.

Happiness overcame her. Books appeared everywhere, in branches, under brush, on top of rocks. The princess read everything in sight.

Months passed.

"I must continue on my journey," said the princess as she ventured forward. "I must go through this brush. It looks so thick," she said questioning herself. "It shall surely shorten my journey."

As she ventured into the brush, it became thicker. She trudged on until she came upon a clearing. "Should I continue forward or go back?" she asked herself. "I shall rest here," she said choosing to sit on a clear patch of ground.

"My, the ground feels different," said the princess.

It began to shake underneath her. She stood, wobbling back and forth as the ground began to crack. Thick vines embedded with large thorns began to spread everywhere, twisting together, stirring up dust, taking on the form of an old wretched woman who coughed dust as she spoke. The dust began to form and shape into all her princes.

"Princess, I have come for you. I shall protect and love you always. Trust me, my princess," their voices echoed through the forest.

"No! No!" shouted the princess.

The woman's arms of thorns reached out into the air. "You shall come. You have no choice! You will come, or I will pierce your skin with thorns of poison. You shall die!" The voices were so full of rage, the princess found herself being forced backward.

"No," she yelled as she reached to her heart for her crystal necklace. "Mystical, Spirituality, come now, I seek you—help."

The black shreds of her dress fell to the ground as she slowly caressed her body.

My skin, my skin, is so soft and warm, she thought. She slowly became clothed in a beautiful white gown of pearls adorned with a green cape made of the finest silk. She touched it with her fingertips spreading out the cape.

"It's so beautiful," she said as she turned and turned. "My

hair," she giggled as she turned, for it was sparkling and glowed with a golden hue. It grew to her feet. Her hands were white, emanating a powerful, brilliant, bright light. A crystal clear blue radiated from her eyes, yellow butterflies fluttered about. She became glorious. She laughed and danced as if nothing else existed.

The wretched woman shook with anger and screamed, "You deceived me! You wretched woman! This is not my princess, The Lowly Princess of the Forest. I don't recognize this princess."

The more the princess laughed and danced the more the wretched woman shrieked.

"I've been deceived." She began to shake as the thorns began to drop to the ground. Her vines began to shrink. The princes' voices began to dissolve into thin air. Then there was silence, as the fine white powder formed, clinging to the princess's cape. She strode to the forest, sprinkling the powder on barren ground. Up sprouted glorious flowers and plants. As she continued on, the princess grew sullen, looking within. *I know not of this person under glorious clothes*, she thought. As she continued to walk her sadness deepened until she came upon a dried up river. She dropped to her knees and wept and wept the largest tears that ever existed.

I feel as if I shall never stop weeping, she thought as the tears continued.

Months passed.

She continued to weep. Before she realized it, the tears had flooded the dried up river.

"Oh, my, I am being carried off. My cape, I'm tangled," she thought in fear as she began to struggle. The current pulled her under as she fought and fought to get to the top of the river. She struggled and fought with the gown to keep from drowning in her own sorrow. When she finally freed herself from the cape, she felt lighter.

I must not stop, she thought rising to the top of the river believing the gown was submerged, but it lay next to her afloat.

I must retrieve it, she thought. As she reached for it, she saw that it was no longer white, but a dingy brown. The cape no longer a brilliant green. She realized they no longer belonged to her, that she must let them go. She released her grip as she watched them drift off into the distance.

Suddenly, the river twirled around her in delight, changing into radiant pastel colors, taking on the forms of women, many women, all different shapes and sizes, wings glorious wings, flowing graciously around them, lifting the princess up, cradling her, rocking her, comforting her with gentleness.

She lay silent, absorbing their touch. *I feel so full and loved within. I am strong. I must continue on my journey.* As the angelic women lovingly set her down, she knew they were with her always. The princess fell to her knees. The sounds of bells filled the air. A wondrous harmonious sound filled her ears - bells, so many bells.

"Jingles, Jingles, is that you?"

There, before her, appeared a woman of magnificent features: clear crystal eyes; pure white hair that draped to her feet; extremely long arms and fingers that if wrapped around you would dissolve within.

Flecks of gold fluttered about, lingering throughout the air. Princess Purity, taken aback, gasped in awe for she had never beheld such beauty. Barely able to speak, she asked, "Who are you? Where are you from?" A pure voice of the most exquisite sound, flowed forth from this breathtakingly beautiful creature.

"I am Lady Wisdom, I am from the Land of Recognition. I'm here to take you further on your journey." As the princess looked up into her eyes, she became mesmerized as Lady Wisdom's eyes began to grow larger and larger, clearer and clearer, as if they would devour the princess. Suddenly, the princess's arms began to stretch forward.

"Oh, my," shouted the princess as the force began pulling her off the ground, sucking her through Lady Wisdom's eyes.

"Oh, oh, my body. It feels so small. My hands, my feet, they're so small." She felt her face.

"What happened? Lady Wisdom, Lady Wisdom, where did you go?" she called. She looked around in confusion. "I'm so small. I'm only a child," said the princess. She looked around. Her reflection was everywhere. "I, I, I'm the child," she said. "The reflection I saw is me. I'm that little girl that is so pale, filthy, cold and alone."

She began to shiver looking down at herself. Suddenly her eyes began to blink uncontrollably. Her body began to shake. "Something's happening. I feel so different," she said. Her body twisted as if in a battle. "I'm, I'm being pulled apart. Whoaaaaaaaaa," she cried catching her balance. "There are two of us." As they stopped to catch their breath, the princess spoke, "Don't be afraid. I recognized you. You are me as a child. I would like to help you."

The child looked into the princess's eyes without uttering a word. Princess Purity reached out her hand. The child slowly rested her tiny hand on the princess'.

"We shall journey forward," spoke the princess. They followed a path, until they came upon a hidden forest. As they entered, it began to rain. The rain surrounded them. The princess realized they had entered the rain forest. They must continue forward. All that lay behind them was a thick fog, and as they ventured forward it continued to rain.

"Why, the raindrops are white," said the princess in awe. As the princess reached out her hand to touch the rain, the child lifted her hand. She began to smile. The rain continued.

Months passed.

They came upon a clearing, feeling a sudden warmth.

"Why, look," said the princess. "You are no longer pale, filthy, cold or alone." The child looked down touching herself in disbelief. "I'm no longer filthy," whispered the child as she spoke for the first time.

The tears began to fall. As she opened her mouth to speak, noises of all sorts came flying out of her mouth. She could not believe herself.

"A voice!" she shouted. Louder and louder, "A voice. I have a voice!" she shouted touching the words that hovered in mid air before her. The princess watched in silence for this was the first time she had heard the child speak. The child began dancing among the words. They continued forward, words dancing about everywhere.

Slowly drifting off, as exhaustion set in, they fell into a deep sleep as never before. Weeks passed and suddenly they were awakened. They heard a loud, loud, firm voice. Clenching their hands tighter, they looked up dazed. Both voices, asked, "where, who, what is happening?"

There, in mid air, appeared the face of a man, wrinkled as if he had journeyed through all time with thick, snowy white hair and a beard that flew about as he spoke. His body took on the form of a strong man, as he appeared close, closer, until he stood before them.

"Welcome to the Land of Patience," he said.

"Who, who are you?" asked the princess.

"I am known throughout the land as Father Wiseman. You are to join me on a journey back through time," he said as he reached out his hands. Before they realized what happened, the princess and child's hand became one. A cloud of smoke filled the air as he twirled them around and around. They began to spin wildly, backwards, faster and faster.

"Oh, ohhhh, we're spinning so fast. Shall we ever stop," they shouted. Slowly, the spinning began to taper off. Until they dropped to the ground, dizzy, their heads reeling.

"Where are we?" asked the child.

"Look," spoke Princess Purity, "It's Secret's Castle, the castle we grew up in."

"I see it," spoke the child. "Oh, princess, I was so afraid there. I was never allowed to speak. My voice became frozen in time. King Captive commanded silence or the punishment was harsh. I would shake uncontrollably in terror, retreating to my hiding place, afraid to breath for every breathe would be heard, and surely I shall have died. Darkness surrounded me. Then, magic, dragons, princes and winged creatures carried me off to many lands -- The Lands of No Time."

"Yes, I remember," said the princess as she hugged the child. "You're safe now. I shall protect you."

As they looked up at the castle they spoke, "Oh, my, the castle."

Its appearance began to change before they're very eyes. It was no longer the same castle. It began to shrink smaller and smaller until it disappeared. Both drew silent as the tears began to fall, tears of all sizes, as if never to stop, until suddenly their vision began to clear.

The haze lifted everything surrounding them took on new shapes and forms. A freshness filled the air. Light absorbed the darkness. The sounds of bells lingered in the air.

"Oh, my," the excitement filled the princess and the child.

"Look, look, it's Mystical, Spirituality, Clarity, Lady Wisdom, Father Wiseman. They've returned," said the princess to the child. The princess became overwhelmed with emotion. She was unable to contain herself. The child listened, afraid to move because she might miss something.

"You've returned," spoke the princess. "I'm so happy. My heart feels as if it will burst. I was so afraid. I was lost deep within the forest. I knew I would never find my way home, when you, the great teachers, appeared teaching me great stories of respect, love, forgiveness. Your words echoed in my mind. *You are worthy, trust, look deep within yourself.* You comforted and guided me in my great time of need. How shall I ever repay you for such wonderful gifts? I, I, I..."

Before the princess could finish, the great teachers' voices intertwined, echoing: "You shall give of the gifts you have received to all who shall enter your path."

"No, No, please do not leave. Please stay," said the princess as their voices began to slowly dissolve.

"We shall be with you always," the teachers said.

The ground began to tremble underneath them. The princess and child struggled to hold onto each other. The sky began to drastically change colors. The great teachers began forming into one great shape until there before them stood The Great Robed Man of Thorns, radiant to behold, adorned by a glorious golden light, his presence strong, radiating compassion, his eyes filled with unspoken words, holding in his hand a heart, beating with a strength so powerful that heat surged through the princess and child's body.

Suddenly, within their hands, appeared a heart filled with so much love and warmth it pulsated. Within its center, there before them, appeared the face of The Great Man of Thorns. The princess was filled with emotion for knowing truth. Tears of joy flowed from their eyes.

Their voices became one, saying, "Thank you for my gifts of suffering, anger, sorrow, joy, forgiveness, compassion, laughter, knowledge, wisdom." The more they spoke of thanks, the stronger the heart began to pulsate. It grew larger and larger with every beat.

As the air filled with crystal drops of white and green, their eyes became mesmerized by the sights that lay before them. The symphony of bells lingered in the air. Their interwoven hands and palms were suddenly filled with such a tremendous warmth. The heart began to dance, separate, radiate through their arms - their bodies. In a sudden swoop, the heart filled their chest from within. They embraced their chests.

"My heart, my heart is weeping white tears, tears of pure joy," they said in unison. They began to laugh, sing and dance. Dewdrops filled the air. Little flickering hearts began dancing about. Happiness consumed them. They danced and danced and danced and danced, until their feet could no longer hold them up.

"My, I'm out of breath," spoke the princess in exhaustion.

"Me, too," said the child as they sat back. "I'm so happy Princess Purity. I feel so safe. My heart," said the child, laying her tiny hand upon her chest, feeling the beat, not knowing words to finish her sentence.

"Oh, Princess Purity, I am so afraid, afraid you shall forget me, that you will leave me alone," said the child. The princess hugged the girl, "Child, I will never leave you alone. I shall always carry you here," she said as she placed her hand upon her chest, "in my heart."

"I shall keep you safe and protect you on your journey."

"Thank you, I must rest now," spoke the child, her eyes becoming heavier and heavier. As she spoke, her voice became smaller and smaller, her body forming into a green mist as she circled around the princess. The princess turned around and around as the mist consumed her being until she became lightheaded. Feeling faint, she had to sit. All of the sudden, she heard bells - whimsical bells - louder and louder - bells, bells - was all she could hear.

"Jingles, Jingles, it must be Jingles, Jingles, are you there?" asked the princess.

"Hah, I'm back," said Jingles wiggling his little body. He was so excited he somersaulted all around before landing in the palm of Princess Purity's hands.

"Oh, Jingles, Jingles," she said stuttering from the excitement. "I'm so happy to see you. I have so much to tell you."

"Time, time, time," he exclaimed as he danced around. "I have plenty of time," he said as he leaned back, propping himself firmly in the princess's hands.

"Jingles, I met myself as a child on my journey. I did not recognize her. She was so filthy. Then the reflection. I saw her. I could no longer deny her existence. She joined me on my journey. We were so afraid, Jingles. Creatures, snakes, little men and books, we journeyed forward together with the help of the Great Teachers of the Forest. Then, then she disappeared.
Oh, Jingles, shall I ever see her again?"

Green radiated from within as she spoke. "Jingles, I'm green. Green is coming from within my soul." Jingles somersaulted through the air as the princess looked down at the palms of her hands. There, she saw the reflection of the child.

"She's here. She's here, within. She's part of me." Suddenly the green began to slowly dissolve, as the princess grew taller and taller. Her voice changed, became stronger.

"Jingles, where are you? I've grown. Jingles, look," she said as she touched herself. "My gown, it's a beautiful pearl white. My hair, it shines. Oh, Jingles, I've changed so."

The princess became silent, absorbing the differences.

"Jingles, shall I ever see the child again?"

"Why, yes, princess she shall be with you always. She is resting for now. It has been a long journey. When you long to find her just look deep within."

"Oh, Jingles, I missed you so."

He danced with joy at these words.

"Jingles, long ago I heard great stories of a land deep, deep within the forest, so rich in color, with beautiful fields; tall green trees that sweep across the land and crystal clear waterfalls. They say, when the wind blows, it sounds as if chimes are singing songs to the heart through the breezes. The sun sparkles through the clouds as if crystals were hung from the sky radiating magnificent colors. Stories say, the land surrounds the most magnificent palace, glorious to behold. They call it Freedom's Palace," said the princess, her eyes twinkling with wonder and curiosity.

"I must journey forward, deep, deep in search of this magnificent land."

Jingles began to giggle in delight. As he wiggled his little body the bells rung out through the forest for everyone to hear. "Princess, princess, I am so proud of you. You are strong. Remember always to trust yourself. Have faith. When your journey twist and turns, look deep within. You shall find the answers."

"Oh, Jingles, thank you. You are truly a friend."

Jingles kissed the princess on the cheek and whispered, "I shall be with you always."

He disappeared, and there, before her, lay a bell, still jingling. She picked it up and smiled. "I shall carry you with me always," she said softly, "as I continue on my journey, in search of Freedom's Palace."

Printed in the United States
1509600001B/16-18